PERNIX

The

Adventures

of a

Small Dinosaur

Dieter Wiesmüller

COBBLEHILL BOOKS

Dutton   New York

It is early in the morning. The first sunbeams fall through the trees of the ancient forest. Pernix, the small dinosaur, is already up and hunting for food.

Pernix was all alone. When he and the four other little dinosaurs had hatched, their parents disappeared. The little dinosaurs had no one to protect them, and all but Pernix were killed by larger animals in the forest. Since that time Pernix wanted to belong to the big ones, so no one could ever harm him.

It was very hard for Pernix to find enough to eat to grow big. But over there! Behind a tree Pernix discovered something—a big insect. It won't be an easy catch because it can fly, and flies in zigzags.

Finally, after a long chase, the insect settled down to rest. Carefully Pernix approached it. Only three more steps...two ...one...and it is snatched away by someone else. Rips, a flying dinosaur, got it!

Pernix ran after the flying dinosaur, but Rips flew high up into the trees. Raps and Rops, his brothers, awaited him eagerly, and they all shared the good catch.

Pernix hears them cackle and shriek. Envious, he looks up at them. Then he has a thought. "Since I am so small, I need help with hunting. They are small, too, but not alone. Maybe they can help me with hunting."

With that in mind, Pernix decides to stay on in their hunting grounds.

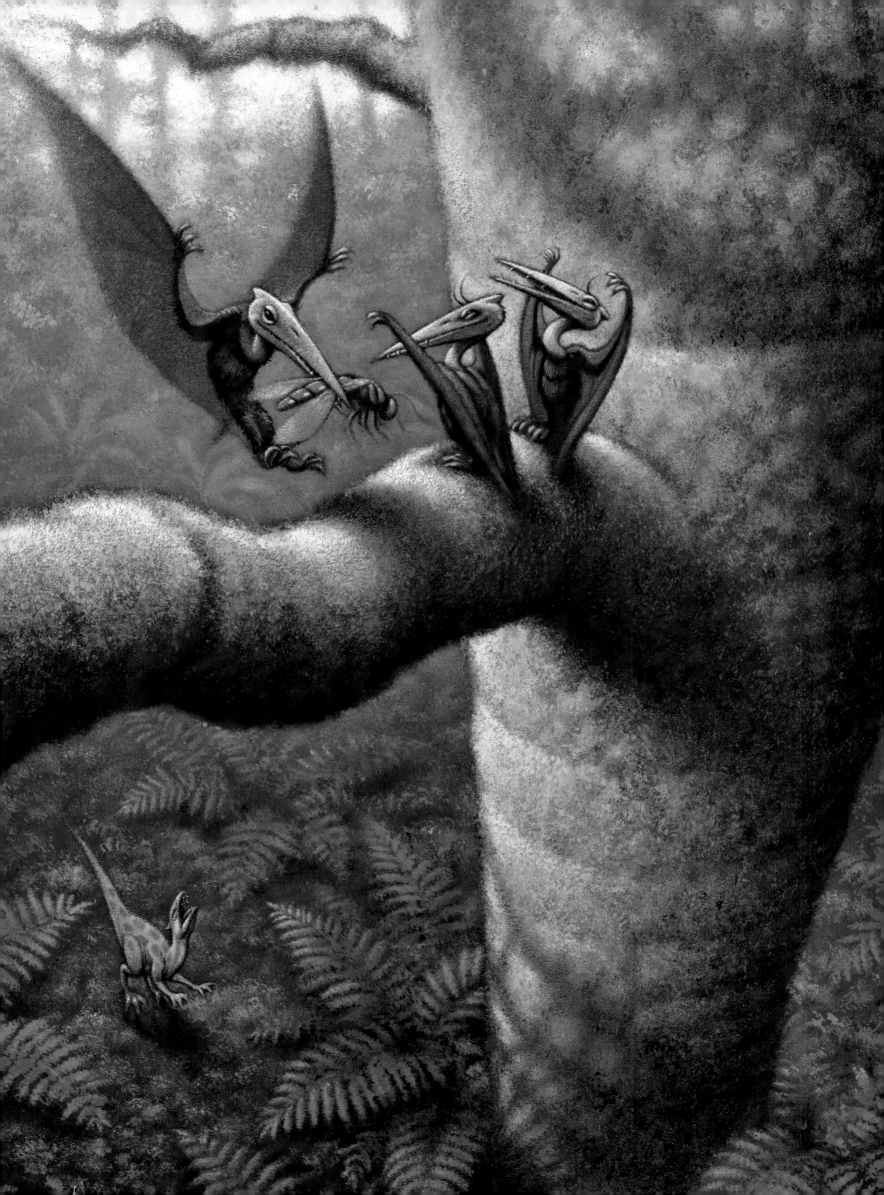

At first it seemed as if things would work out between Pernix and the flying dinosaurs. The four of them hunted together and found quite a lot of food.

But when it came to eating, Rips, Raps, and Rops didn't want
Pernix to share. Every time they quarreled with him. And then they
decided to get rid of him.

They want Pernix to leave their
hunting grounds, but Pernix won't
leave. He is as hungry as ever. So
the three brothers decide on an
evil plan.

Rips, Raps, and Rops lead
Pernix to the river. "There are
delicious frogs," they say. Pernix
is very surprised when the three of
them suddenly go flying off.

But then he understands.
Before Pernix can get any frogs,
what had looked like a log
suddenly becomes the opening of
a huge mouth. The crocodile
almost gets him!

"I wonder if I could eat creatures with teeth—creatures like Rips, Raps, and Rops," thinks Pernix. "But I would have to be bigger to catch them first."

Pernix is very sad. Nobody is as alone as he is, not even the giant dinosaurs. "Bigger! I have to get bigger!" But right now it is only his hunger that has gotten bigger.

Pernix finds a nest with eggs. Nobody is guarding it. He loves eggs! But a sound in the forest makes him alert. Something is coming. It is Torvus, a fierce hunter. Torvus is a little bigger than Pernix, but he is also alone. "Perhaps he will help me hunting."

Torvus is getting closer. Pernix can hear his stomach grumble.
Torvus is hungry too! "Maybe he is hunting me and wants to eat
me," Pernix thinks. Frightened, he sneaks away, leaving the nest
with the eggs to Torvus.

"How can I grow if I never get enough to eat?" As always, Pernix is hungry and feels very lonely.

He sees a caterpillar. He wants to have that caterpillar. But again he hears something in the forest.

A dinosaur, as small as Pernix, is approaching the caterpillar from the other side. Does it want the caterpillar too? But Pernix wants that prey for himself—and only for himself. He snatches one end of it.

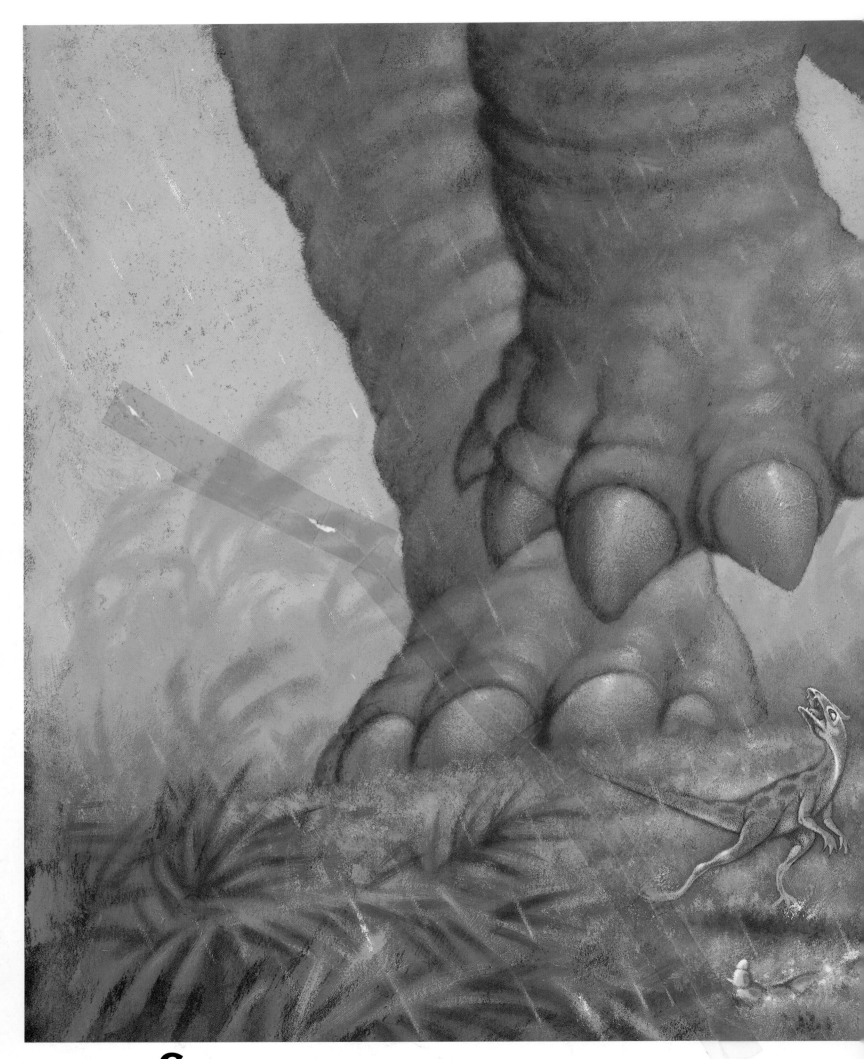

Suddenly the ground starts shaking. The stamping sound of giant dinosaur feet fills the forest.

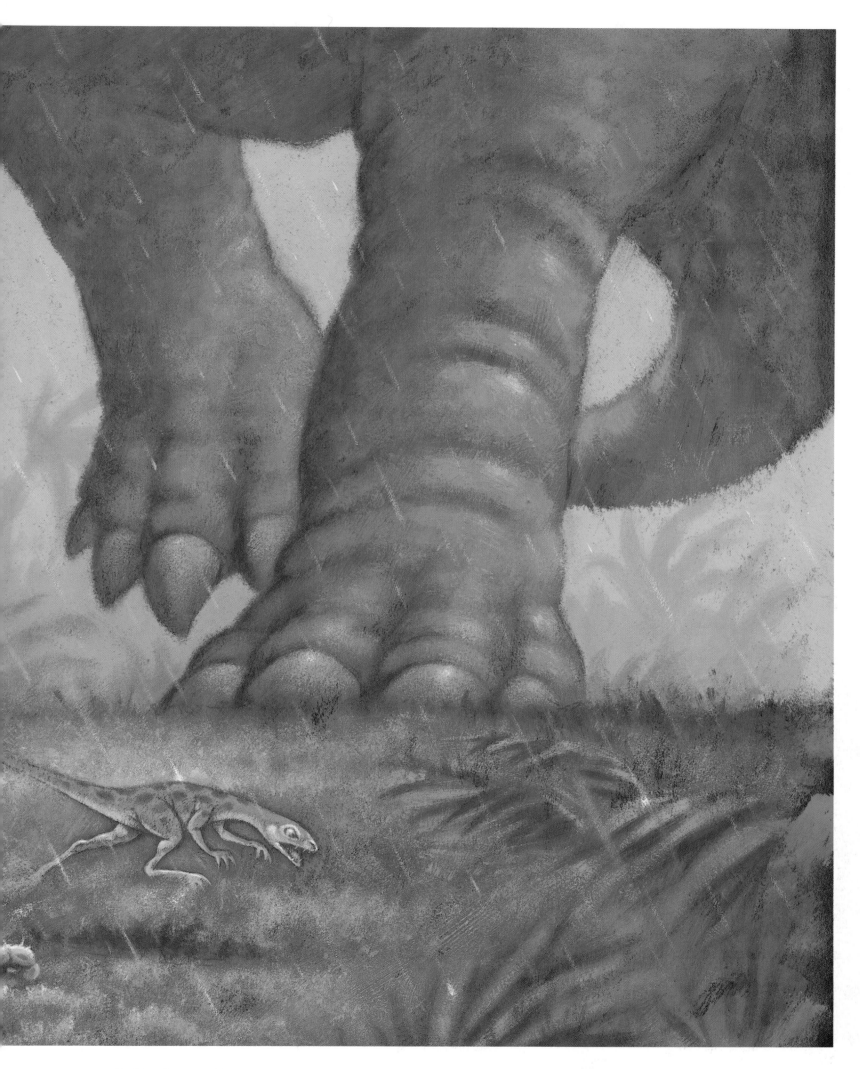

Both small dinosaurs forget their hunger and run away in panic.
Left is only the fat caterpillar.

Pernix has never seen such a huge dinosaur before. He feels very small, and he is alone with his empty stomach—except for the little thief, who looks just like him.

It is now raining very heavily and both are very cold. Viva, the other little dinosaur, carefully approaches Pernix. She comes closer and closer. Soon they are together—and then they are warm.

Huddled close together, Pernix and Viva are not cold anymore. They decide to stay together, even after the rain has stopped. They start hunting together, and soon they are so skillful that they have plenty of food.

Months go by, and Pernix has forgotten that he wanted to get as big as the giant dinosaurs. He is no longer hungry, and he is no longer alone. But what is Viva up to now? he wonders.

Viva is looking for a hiding place to build a nest. At first, Pernix just watches her, but then he starts to help her. And then there are five beautiful eggs in the nest.

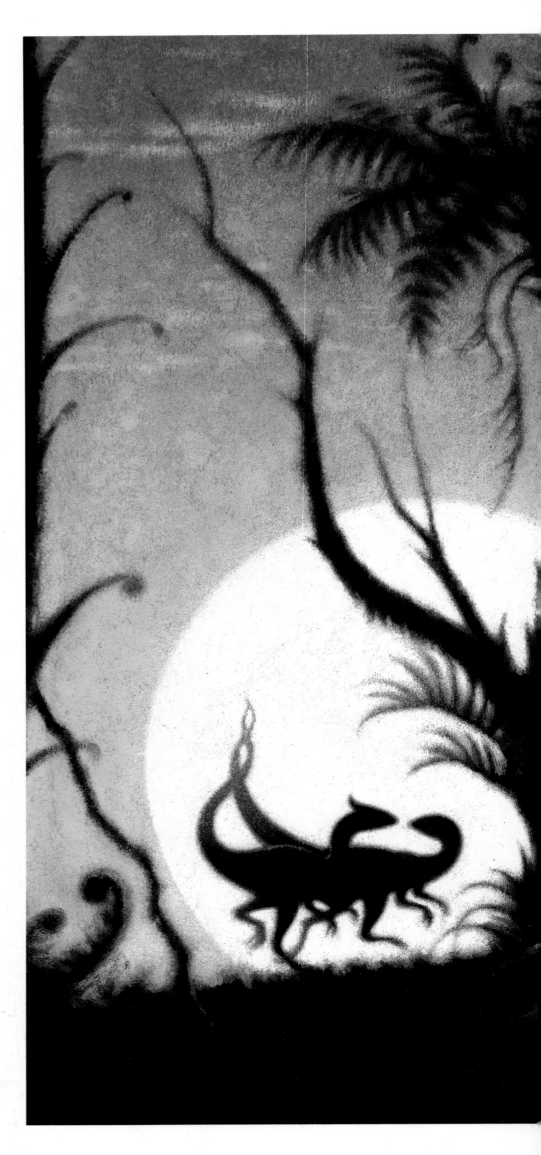

Viva and Pernix guard their nest all the time. They are afraid somebody will steal the eggs. But soon five young dinosaurs are hatching.

Will they get as big as we are, wonders Pernix. Maybe they won't get any bigger at all. There are thieves all around. Most of the time you can't see them, and sometimes not even hear them. It is a dangerous time for the young dinosaurs. But they are lucky. Their parents take good care of them.

One morning Pernix and Viva and the little dinosaurs wake up to a very loud noise. It is the huge green dinosaur and her young. She is taller than a big tree.

Fortunately, giant dinosaurs like this one are vegetarians. But even so, Viva and Pernix and their young have to leave quickly if they don't want to get run over by her.

Finally they find a new place to stay. Hopefully, they will have some peace and quiet now.

Suddenly they hear loud shrieks. Pernix recognizes them immediately. It is Rips, Raps, and Rops. The three brothers have seen the young dinosaurs and eye them hungrily.

Once again they devise a wicked plan. Their noise has attracted Torvus, who has been close by. They decide that Torvus will get rid of Pernix and Viva, so that Rips, Raps, and Rops can get to the young dinosaurs.

But before Torvus discovers the hiding place, Pernix appears in front of him and lures him away from the nest.

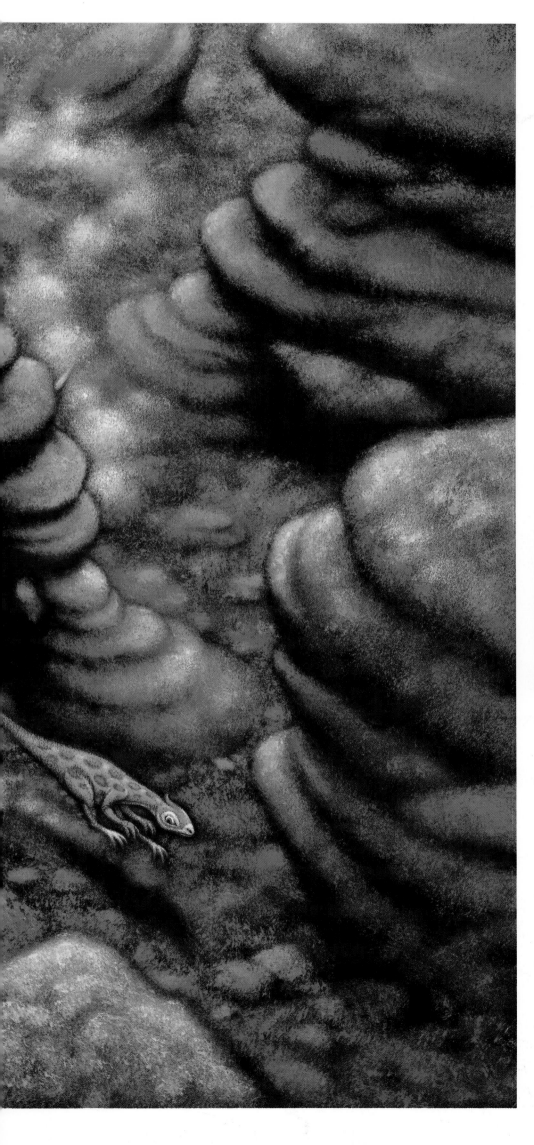

Immediately Torvus starts chasing Pernix. They run out of the forest onto flat rocky land. It is a very long chase. Pernix has been able to lure Torvus away from the nest, but now it's time to save his own life! Torvus is bigger than he is and not willing to give up easily. "Why am I so small?" Pernix cries, and he jumps over a big boulder to find a hiding place. Torvus jumps after him, and at the same moment . . .

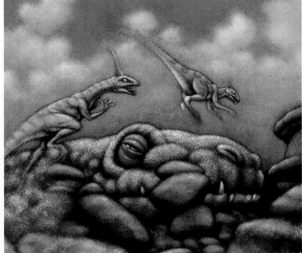

...both are thrown high up into the air and land in front of a giant flesh-eating dinosaur. The giant greedily snaps after the larger prey—Torvus—and Pernix has time to escape.
"How lucky I am to be the smaller one! He didn't see me," Pernix thinks. "But now I have to get back to Viva and the young dinosaurs because Rips, Raps, and Rops are still there."

Finally Pernix is back at the nest. He sees that Viva is trying to chase the three flying dinosaurs away. But every time she gets rid of one, another is already back to attack.

With one big jump, Pernix is right in the middle of them. Now he has giant strength—like a big dinosaur. He bites the flying dinosaurs and won't let go. Frightened and shrieking loudly, they flee. The fight is over, but Pernix has gotten one of them.

The young dinosaurs quickly learn that creatures with teeth can be eaten. They hungrily attack the prey.

It is nighttime and in the trees small furry animals, which come out only in darkness, are searching for food.

Lately the moon has become bigger again. Not so Pernix and Viva, but their young ones have grown. They are not hungry anymore and all have fallen asleep, close to one another.

Even in this gigantic ancient forest, it is much better not to be alone, no matter how big or how small you are.